ANN M. MARTIN

BABY-SITTERS LITTLE SISTER®

KAREN'S WITCH

A GRAPHIC NOVEL BY

KATY FARINA

WITH COLOR BY BRADEN LAMB

graphix

An Imprint of

SCHOLASTIC

For Laura Elizabeth, the newest Perkins
A. M. M.

For Maddie, my own little sister
K. F.

Library of Congress Control Number: 2019933276

ISBN 978-1-338-35611-3 (hardcover)
ISBN 978-1-338-31519-6 (paperback)

10 9 8 7 6 5 4 3 2 1   20 21 22 23 24

Printed in Malaysia   108
First edition, January 2020

Edited by Cassandra Pelham Fulton and David Levithan
Book design by Phil Falco and Shivana Sookdeo
Publisher: David Saylor

CHAPTER 1

My name is Karen Brewer.

I'm six going on seven years old, and I think I'm very lucky.

I'm lucky because my little brother, Andrew, and I have two families!

Are you ready for a weekend at Daddy's house?

Yup.

Andrew

Mommy and Daddy got divorced, and then married other people. So now I have lots of twos!

Toys →

Tickly (my special blanket) ↑

Pairs of jeans ↑

Party shoes ↖

1

Andrew and I live at the big house every other weekend.

The big house is noisy and busy, and someone is always there to play with me.

Also...

A witch lives next door.

I know she's a witch because I spy on her all the time.

Daddy's rule is NO SPYING, but I can't help it!

A witch is scary but interesting.

The witch says her name is Mrs. Porter...

But I call her **Morbidda Destiny.**

Smells funny

Wispy gray hair

Long black robes

Herb garden for spells

Midnight

6

11

MEOW!
MEOW!

Is that coming
from the front door?

That's Boo-Boo.
I'll let him in.

AAAAHHH!

CHAPTER 2

15

Midnight? So what? He probably just wants to play with Boo-Boo.

But, Kristy, that's the witch's cat! Or maybe the witch herself!

And he's blinking at me.

I know he's here to put me under a spell!

Maybe Morbidda Destiny wants to turn **me** into a cat!

Why would she want to do that?

CLICK!

Let's finish our game.

Andrew and David Michael are waiting for us.

SHIVER
SHUDDER

Kristy, I'm scared.

Oh, Karen, it will be all right. Really.

What took you so long?

FOR YOUR INFORMATION...

It was **not** Boo-Boo at the door.

Who was it, then?

It was... **Midnight!**

Morbidda Destiny's cat?!

You guys, what's the big deal?

The big deal is that a witch's cat...

Or the witch herself...

Was on our front porch. Midnight has never come over here before.

I wonder why he chose tonight?

Maybe because it's a full moon.

The wind is blowing.

It's a witchy, autumny night.

I think you're scaring your brother.

Kristy, let's not play Old Maid anymore. Let's read stories!

But not witch stories.

I **want** witch stories!

I know a witch story that's not scary. It's called **The Tooth Witch.**

It's about a good witch who becomes the tooth fairy.

That sounds boring.

Now I want another witch story!

Not me, no more witch stories.

Me neither, no more stories **at all**.

It's bedtime anyway.

Go on upstairs and brush your teeth. All three of you.

And, Karen, when you're ready for bed, I'll read you **The Littlest Witch**.

Deal?

Deal!

Everyone
hop into bed!

Are you ready for your bedtime story?

Once upon a time, there u

But all the other witches...

And the l black kitt

CHAPTER 3

Too spooky!

CLICK!

Karen, what are you doing?

Nothing!

Morbidda Destiny is a witch. That's a fact.

I've seen her in her witchy black clothes lots of times.

I've seen her funny hair.

I've seen her herbs. And I've seen her broom.

But do you want to know something strange?

I've never seen her **ride** a broom.

All witches ride brooms.

29

Maybe witches only ride brooms at night.

That would make sense. If they rode them in daytime, people would see them.

I'll watch Morbidda Destiny's house until I see her get on her broomstick.

Then I'll call Kristy.

When Kristy sees Mrs. Porter riding a broom, she will finally believe that she's a true witch.

35

Let me tell you a story.

Once upon a time...

CHAPTER 4

All quiet.

Good morning!

Good morning!

Where's Daddy?

He's out front, working in the garden.

Smooch!

41

Still nothing.

Karen?

What are you doing?

Looking at Morbidda Destiny's house.

You know what? I don't think she's home.

So?

I don't think she ever came back after she flew off last night. And you know what that means, right?

What?

It means she's at a witch meeting.

Something is going to happen.

Soon.

Karen, Karen, Karen.

Kristy, Kristy, Kristy.

HAHA! HAHA! HAHA! HAHA! HAHA!

TA-DA!

We need Boo-Boo. We have to make him sit on one of the brooms.

There he is!

RUSTLE RUSTLE

Peek...

Heh heh heh!

Oh no...

CHAPTER 5

I know what I'm doing is spying.

I can't help it.

I just **have** to hear what Morbidda Destiny is saying.

RUSTLE RUSTLE

Still hidden. Whew!

Midnight.

Twelve o'clock.

SLAM!!

Hannie, this is terrible!

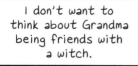
I don't want to think about Grandma being friends with a witch.

Oh, I don't, um, like herbs.

Please don't grow them, Daddy. They're gross.

Come on, Hannie. Let's go to my room.

That was close. I didn't want Daddy to know we've been spying.

But, oh, Hannie, just think. Tonight at midnight a whole flock of witches is going to be right next door!

CHAPTER 6

Bedtime!

Daddy? Can Kristy come up and read me a story?

I'll ask her.

STEP
STEP
STEP

Good night.

Don't let the bedbugs bite.

See you in the morning light.

Good night, Karen.

SMOOCH!

Good night, Moosie.

SMOOCH!

Oh, goody!

Can you read **The Littlest Witch**, please?

Again?

Why do you want to hear it? It always scares you.

Okay, then. **Little Toot.**

Do you want to sleep in my room again? You look scared.

Boy witches?!

I–I'm not scared.

You sure **look** scared.

Well, I'm not.

Besides...

I have a plan.

I can't do my plan in Kristy's room.

Thank you for asking, though.

I'll be fine.

All right.

Good night, then.

And good night, Moosie.

Good night, Kristin Amanda Thomas!

Yes! There we go!

This is my plan:

The alarm clock will wake me up before midnight.

Gasp!

Morbidda Destiny must have put a spell on it.

She must have figured out my plan!

I bet she put a spell on the whole neighborhood, too.

Something to keep us all asleep.

That's the only way to hold a witch meeting, of course.

That Morbidda Destiny is just too smart.

I wonder what happened at the meeting.

What did they talk about? What did they decide?

There's only one way to find out:

Spy.

Without getting caught.

Today's my last chance for two weeks. Mommy's picking up Andrew and me soon.

Today is going to be a **big** day.

CHAPTER 7

Karen!

Hi!

What are you doing back here?

Oh. I, um, I...

I'm back here looking for my ring! That beautiful ring from the cereal box.

I know Daddy will remember that ring. Andrew and I had a big fight over it. We both wanted it.

That's too bad, honey.

Oh well, maybe I'll get another one sometime. Thanks for helping me look!

Whew!

Another close call.

As soon as Daddy leaves...

I can go back to spying.

Still quiet.

Quiet as a tombstone.

Tombstone.

Now that's a scary word.

I wonder why I thought about tombstones.

Let's see. Graveyards... misty nights...ghosts...

Augh!

Oh, there's Mary Anne and her dad.

Gotta go, see you later! And quit spying!

Daddy's going to the backyard?

Perfect.

Now I can spy from the front.

What is she doing?

Oh.

She's sweeping the steps.

BRUSH

Do they really need to be swept?

Maybe she's trying to make people forget that she's a witch.

Now she has hedge clippers?

SNIP SNIP

Oh.

A bouquet.

Hmm.

She's just cutting more herbs and talking to Daddy.

Hmmmm.

Sweeping the steps... Cutting flowers and herbs...

She seems to be getting ready for something...but what?

But with witches, it's hard to tell.

I need Hannie!

Right now!

They're bringing food and books and papers. The books must be spell books, and the papers must have spells written on them.

New spells that they need to practice!

Are you sure?

Yes! And you know what?

We have to go over there.

We have to stop the meeting.

We have to **save our neighborhood!**

Can't someone else do it?

No one else knows about the meeting.

Besides, don't you want to be a hero?

The mayor would give us a parade. Maybe even medals!

The mayor would give everyone a day off from school, too.

That would be fun...

But you don't want to go to Morbidda Destiny's house, do you?

That would be crazy! They'll be practicing spells! You said so!

They'll probably put a spell on us!

Then we'll protect ourselves!

Before we go into the witch's house, we'll go to her garden.

We'll cut some herbs and take them with us.

I don't know...

And we'll make up our own spell. A spell to use against witches!

Oh, Karen...

What?

This doesn't sound like a good idea. That's all. It sounds dangerous!

Hannie. Don't we always decide to use my ideas?

Yes.

And isn't it always okay?

NO!

Remember that time you said the Delaneys have so many flowers in their yard, they'd never miss just one?

So we dug one up, and Mrs. Delaney caught us, and we got in trouble!

Well...

What about the time you said, "Let's spray Noodle with perfume. It will make his dog smell go away!" Remember that?

We used Mommy's good perfume, and Noodle smelled awful, even after two baths!

Aww, Hannie, I was just --

Besides, what do you know about witch spells and herbs?

Plenty. I live next to a witch, don't I?

Yes.

Believe me, I know enough.

Now, are you going to help me? Are you going to save our neighborhood and be a hero?

I guess...

Great! Let's go!

Wait, let me tell Mommy and Daddy!

Don't you tell them anything!

We just need to take a few leaves.

Which ones?

Spells always say things like a speck of cinnamon or a pinch of, oh, say, garlic.

How do we know which ones we need? And how do we know which is which?

Stop asking so many questions. Any old leaves will do.

But what about the magic? Aren't these magic herbs?

Of course. That's why they'll protect us. Now go get some stuff!

Me?! You go!

They smell funny.

Never mind that. Put them on the ground while we make a spell.

We'll give them a **whack**?!

I just mean with our spell. We won't really hit them.

Now come on, we have to learn the spell fast!

If there's any trouble at Morbidda Destiny's, this is what we'll do.

First, we'll put the herbs in our pockets.

If there's trouble, touch the herbs with one hand.

With the other hand, hold on to me tight.

Then we say our spell together. Okay?

Okay.

How does the spell go again?

Here are the witches, we'll give them a whack, so they can't hurt us, and never come back.

Now, are you ready?

...What are we doing first?

We're going to walk over to Morbidda Destiny's house and ring her bell.

When she answers the door, we'll march right into the meeting.

We will?

I'm pretty scared.

Karen, let's go.

Hannie, look at all those cars.

Think of how many witches and warlocks are inside Morbidda Destiny's house right now.

Think of what they might be planning.

We have to go see.

Think of how much trouble we'll be in.

We will **not** get in trouble.

We're going to get a parade and a day off from school. Maybe crowns and medals.

SIGH

Well, I'm not sure about that.

I just need Hannie to come with me.

DING-
DONG!!

Oh no...

Heh heh heh...

Well, what have we here?

Did she say what can I do **to** you?

We would like to go to the party, please.

Ah, certainly.

They seem nice. They look like they're having fun.

Well, of c-course. Witches are always nice to other witches.

It's real people like us who have to worry. So keep your hand on your herbs.

Okay.

Now. I have to make a speech.

Ahem. Ahem. **Ahem.**

AHEM! AHEM!

What?!

No, really.

We...we know the truth.

And H-Hannie and I have come to...to...

Well, if you try to do anything to our neighborhood, we'll...we'll...

Well, um, we might tell our parents...

So...

!!!

Oh no! Hannie, they're going to get us!

Quick! The spell!

Here are the witches.

We'll give them a smack.

Not smack, Hannie. It's **whack!**

I'm sorry.

I hate apologizing.

Let's go.

Now, Hannie, you go straight home, please.

Okay.

As for you, young lady, just what did you think you were doing?

Saving the neighborhood.

KNOCK
KNOCK

Hello?

Watson? Elizabeth?

Mother Packett?

Let me tell you what your daughter has just done.

Hello, Mrs. ...

Mm-Mm!!

I need to return to the meeting now.

I hope my friends won't laugh at me too much.

CLICK!

Karen Brewer, I hope you can explain yourself.

Is Karen going to get in trouble now?

All right, kids. Go find something to do. Watson and I need to talk to Karen alone.

You better tell us the story from the beginning.

Even after everything that happened, I know that Mrs. Porter really is a witch.

Maybe she really did have a gardening meeting.

But she's still a witch.

After all, didn't I see her fly away on a broom?

ANN M. MARTIN'S The Baby-sitters Club is one of the most popular series in the history of publishing — with more than 176 million books in print worldwide — and inspired a generation of young readers. Her novels include *Belle Teal*, *A Corner of the Universe* (a Newbery Honor book), *Here Today*, *A Dog's Life*, and *On Christmas Eve*, as well as the much-loved collaborations, *P.S. Longer Letter Later* and *Snail Mail No More*, with Paula Danziger, and *The Doll People* and *The Meanest Doll in the World*, written with Laura Godwin and illustrated by Brian Selznick. She lives in upstate New York.

KATY FARINA is a comics artist and illustrator based in Los Angeles. She's currently a background painter on *She-Ra and the Princesses of Power* at DreamWorks TV. In the past, she's done work for BOOM! Studios, Oni Press, and Z2 Comics. Visit her online at katyfarina.com.

DON'T MISS THE BABY-SITTERS CLUB GRAPHIC NOVELS!